Who has the keys

Who has the keys

by Shawn Michael Sullivan

ISBN 9780998520551

Neon Burrito Publishing
The truth of the book is the book alone

CONTENTS

I

Isabelle

Owing to reality's expansive possibilities, and the complex number of things that can happen in life, her biography said, "Girl of your memes," his biography said, "But who will write about you," she was visiting from Auckland, New Zealand, he lived in Los Angeles, America, and they became aware of each other through a dating application on their smartphones.

She was visiting where he was living, and so he sent a message to ask when she was leaving.

One last day here, she replied.

Hmmm, he thought, indeed, and thus suggested a simple afternoon guided tour of Fairfax Avenue, from Beverly Boulevard to Melrose Boulevard, as he was familiar with his neighborhood and wouldn't have to drive.

She was like sure, cool.

So around two p.m. on the first Saturday in January they met at the Shell Station on the corner of Fairfax and Beverly: she sat waiting by a fountain, wearing a black jumpsuit, black sandals, and carrying a dark moss green jacket; he approached her wearing a pink sweater, black jeans and yellow sneakers.

And this all happened because she was born, he was born, both their parents were born, and everybody before that was born too.

Her parents Peranakan, she, thirty-two year-old Isabelle, had been born in Australia, bred in a New Zealand suburb, and given her name from a book of recommendations her mother consulted, while his Appalachian grandparents had settled in the heart of America so he, Brett, was a thirty-four year-old second-generation Ohioan, bred in the country, and given a basic name that seemed like a good idea around the time he was born for some reason only God remembers.

What also needed to and did take place before their meeting was human evolution and the founding of nations, the integration of sidewalks into urban planning, the invention of airplanes, the blossoming of dating services as a business concept, and the sociotechnological development of smartphones, plus much-much more and, you get it, anyway, she and he had to first meet at the Shell Station for them to first meet at the Shell Station like they did, such that, as planned, he told her about his neighborhood: That is CBS Television City, where *The Price Is Right* is taped, and also *The Late Late Show with James Corden*, who was in Mike Leigh's *All or Nothing* by the way; that is a statue of Raoul Wallenberg, a Swede who saved Jewish lives in Hungary during World War II; Tyler, the Creator owns this clothing store, Golf, which was once across the street and named Odd Future; that is the Supreme Store; that is RipNDip; these are on-trend street wear stores; there are two full-on sneaker stores; and that is Canter's Deli, with a Jewish mural facing its parking lot; in the recent past this was a Jewish neighborhood.

For conversational purposes they also discussed notable New Zealand cultural successes, such as pop sensation Lorde, and movie writer/director Taika Waititi (Isabelle considered *Boy* the best New Zealand movie ever made). A phenomenon of Aotearoa herself, Isabelle had founded an intellectual cultural website, and curated contemporary Asian art for national and city events. By helping her community appreciate and understand art she was part of the good fight; she lived an art life on an island country, had successful art friends, and took international holidays and summer excursions.

Isabelle seemed extra lovely at the Fairfax District in Los Angeles right then. Brett asked if she always felt lovely or if she was in a particularly good mood. She replied that she was always like this (and Brett was not yet familiar with vague nervous energy instigated by existentialism in a Western world beta future).

Brett was a big dumb dreamer whose life was a good idea according to just him, although nobody knows anything so what the hell. He was an absolute unit of trash and chandelier culture—the lows and highs of cinema and literature, without a goddamn thing from the in-between—and he worked as a freelance art department production assistant, although his main hustle was as a writer/director of no budget movies, with his recent short film *The Universe is a Water Person* a Vimeo Staff Pick, which minor life success opened Isabelle to liking him that day maybe, or was why she gave him a chance probably, because she caught him on a good day among so many indifferent ones, if you know what I mean, based on life being like that, with better things bringing better things, and Brett always the same.

She was a go-getter who conquered reality's cruelty with her winning can-do attitude, and he was a deplorable malcontent who endured life while accomplishing little.

His guess had been that he would show her around his neighborhood and that would be that.

By the time they were French kissing at a booth in the Kibitz Room he recognized something special taking place.

There had been significant indications.

Her hair tucked behind her ear, she wore nice earrings he noticed, and mhm he listened while she mentioned that when younger she wrote about a succubus falling in love with a man she couldn't kill.

In the back alley he grabbed her ass and what do you think happened next.

The movie *Chungking Express* lit his bedroom as they learned about each other through a night they let last as long as they could, as she was flying back to Auckland the next day.

The night lasted until sunrise, and then she was gone from there but not from him.

On the plane over the ocean she texted him that if
time had permitted she would have married him downtown as he had suggested their night together that
seemed as if a dream they agreed, although his agree-
ment went unspoken, as he did not text her back right
then, since she lived over there, and he lived over here,
so their relationship wasn't possible he realized.

Though how wonderful their one night together had
been, and how wonderful his thoughts of her remained.

A few days passed by and neither did he text her
back after she texted her email address *for emergencies*,
because he figured she was sending her email address
solely for emergencies, as still she lived there and he
lived here (ocean of a difference). Though then a couple more days passed by and—amid his dreamlike
memories of her—she texted about listening to music
that played their night together, Faye Wong's *"夢中人"*
from *Chungking Express*, and well then he felt com-
pelled to mention that he listened to music from that
night too: The xx, their eponymous album.

And as a consequence of their connection beginning,
she called him once while they shared a texting session,
without mentioning her call beforehand, which

abruptness he considered a bold touch in terms of
mating rituals, and later he called her too. It was a natural process, animal magnetism to say it one way, or
quantum entanglement to say it another scientific way
that might better describe the force of attraction they
felt themselves experiencing.

Even while she lived over there and he lived over
here they came to know and grow close to each other
through phone conversations in which they noticed
their different types of lives. She would often ask him
specific questions: can you name five good things that
happened to you last year; can you name your role
model?

Good things? Role models? She made him concentrate. He was coerced into learning about his love lan-
guage, his Myers–Briggs Type, and developing a more
expansive understanding of his astrological sign (Pisces
of course).

Brett mentioned his darkness to her, and he empha-
sized for clarity.

Alive to the present, she felt herself sung to by him,
and he felt himself sung to by her. When one makes
sense to another person it helps the whole world make
sense.

Did they want to dream together longer?

They felt there was no other option.

Thus in the following days he called her from his car at night (away from his roommate) for hour or longer phone dates that led to them becoming boyfriend and girlfriend, and calling each other in the morning as well.

After the first month of their extraordinary long-distance relationship, he suggested that she see her friends for her approaching birthday, so her friends wouldn't think he was guarding her, but she said she wanted to spend the night with him, so she spent her birthday night on the phone with him (which he adored and felt lucky about).

And soon there was phone sex and the dream was so bright she had plane tickets to Los Angeles, and that was a lot plus nowhere near a description of everything that happened between them, which is very much how this story of them will go.

His birthday one weekend after hers, the weekend after his own birthday he first encountered what lived beyond the lights of their dream together: "I can't get everything from one person," she said to him during her first work event (a K-Pop dance show) that took place during their relationship. And she meant that he wasn't saying or doing what she needed him to say or do. "If you could read my thoughts." Before this particular phone conversation she had social media shared her appreciation for a close friend, and Brett was beginning to learn about the narrative that existed outside their relationship, Isabelle's business side and social reality within a community that valued her. He lived a life unrelated to her as well, but his whole perspective was that his dream with her made his life better. That night he had gone to see Jean-Luc Godard's *The Image Book* at the Aero Theatre, and he longed for her through each second of each day that led him to her.

Friction existed between them from the beginning, but movement does create friction. After a short while they began the process of sleeping together through the phone, with attached headphones, and hearing the breathing of sleeping Isabelle became Brett's favorite sound out of all the sounds he ever heard throughout his entire life.

One night Brett walked toward McDonald's on Wilshire Boulevard for a ten-piece chicken nuggets with honey and over the phone he and Isabelle initiated the plan for her first visit. Earlier he had sent Isabelle a link to the song "In the Background" by Lil Zubin, a young Philadelphia musician sharing sad songs with homemade beats, a popular form of music those days, and this either did or did not inspire her to text him that she could visit him for a week at the end of March.

Which she would, even while neither of them knew exactly what they would be like together in person.

Not a poet by trade or talent, still each man carries his own batch of poems, and dear reader forgive Brett for this, because there are real problems in the world: after Isabelle's first visit Brett wrote poetry about his experience—not because he wanted to, or because he felt meant to, but because he felt as if he had to:

isabelle in los angeles: one

she texts me 'no rush'
i'm inching forward in lax traffic
can't rush anyway

then i'm at the terminal looking for her
and i can't find her
so i circle around and search again

and there she is
sitting in the sun
just like she said

we head to our santa monica apartment
and finally my hand is on her thigh
thank god

upon arrival we
enter heaven naked

then sit beside each other over dinner
at the galley
beneath xmas lights in a nautical theme

drinking maker's mark back at our apartment
unknown pleasures on the tv
we're eating sugar cubes

then we're sleeping beside each other and
multiple-times we nighttime wake
for extra kisses

to me she is minor and major beauty
wordless beauty even

it is an understatement to say that the next day

a new and uniquely gorgeous sunlit day began

at a park by the beach we lie on a blanket (her
birthday gift to me) she's reading *lonely asian
woman* and our love is like a love poem

i'm reading poetry she gave me, gregory kan

no matter which outcome
in the dizzying array of all possible futures
no matter the fear
i will meet you there

we eat a four course italian dinner
but that story is being omitted
just like some other stories
are also being omitted

an explanation of omissions
being omitted

at night we
sidewalk stroll our santa monica neighborhood
before turning on *la vie de bohème*
and laughing together in bed the next morning

followed by
cafe 101 and a special cameo

then a road trip
another special cameo
and two full days

with desert sunlight causing me to
lose track of subtlety

she is next to me
and she is far from me

i can't tell what's real and what's imaginary

but then during a fresh night
just the two of us
inside our downtown luxury apartment
we talk about what really matters
how we really matter to each other

and
sleep
wake
kiss
sleep
wake
kiss
this time with background city noises

in the morning we consider the clock rude and
each other marvelous
our hands on each other's bodies

during these days it feels as if
the days are short and life is short

which is
much nicer
than when it feels like
long days in a hard life

we stroll to the last bookstore
then little tokyo's village plaza
we drink sparkling sake in a revolving sushi bar
and hold hands like scuba divers wear regulators

in the afternoon i am on a pink velvet couch
listening to first the music of kendrick lamar and
then khalid while reading more poetry she
brought me, hera lindsay bird

but describing love is a backwards talent
like a bad mental taxidermy
where everything living comes out stuffed

and she is eating cheetos puffs while
working on her computer
stopping work now and then to visit me, kiss me

nothing happening but pure life
there is nothing else that i need

then we are high inside the central library's mar-
ble floored rotunda
a mural cycle on its upper walls, a
zodiac chandelier above us

we eat dinner on a wooden counter
at chicas tacos
before from cvs she buys candy
to bring back to new zealand

i want to marry her

and i am aware of time, which is unaware of me

how long will
she be gone from me once she leaves
i wonder
unrelated to another question

how much she means to me is
plenty

together on the pink velvet couch at night
drinking maker's mark only because we have it
a table lamp is the final decision about our best
other light. in addition to the glowing television

here i am with her and not caring about the
whole rest of the world
seeing a side of her that the rest of the world
does not see

there she is, my everything

sleep
wake
kiss
sleep
wake
kiss
morning

o isabelle
why did you let me suggest carl's jr
for our final morning
and why are you leaving this city?

carl's jr because you love me
leaving la for nz because reality

we're naming dogs in a park
we see the dogs but no one sees our secrets

wait, before then was another park
where we were artists
but anyway next came
chungking express

driving her to lax
i feel blessed
which seems confusing
for a number of reasons
the most obvious being
i'm driving her to lax

she is leaving and
i want to hold her

not ready to leave her, i hold her
so our goodbye takes a while
(still far too brief)

i miss her before she kisses me as i'm about to
drive away
she is gone but not from me

isabelle in los angeles: two

in the evenings while sleeping
we wake to each other's open eyes
and once she said it must be
because of our shifting bodies

so we wake to each other's movements
and we move to each other's lips

her hand on my neck
my hand on her cheek

my right leg across her body
she moves closer to me

and we return to sleep to wake again
being where we want to be

isabelle in los angeles: three

on our way to desert x
a site-specific contemporary art exhibition in
coachella valley

we stop to see my friend
building a house in joshua tree
which i think is neat

and she tells me
she's seen people build houses before

then i hear some comments speculating
about whether this trip will meet her standards

and she has meaningful standards
which i appreciate, so that's important to me

therefore i later ask her how things are
and she says everything is fine

hearing what she says
i wonder about what she doesn't say

so later i ask again if everything is fine
and she replies in the same way

her saying what she did before
makes me feel as i did before: ponderous

then we're at my friend's
joshua tree airbnb

where there is nothing to do
but work on a puzzle
so she works on a puzzle, and she's brilliant at it

us four hanging out,
she seems happy as she can be in this situation
one of her best friends with her,
happy as well it seems

but i wonder
if this is the kind of happiness she wants
and in bed she asks me if anything is wrong

i'm actually trying to figure out
if anything is wrong
so i tell her that nothing is

since nothing that i can or want to explain is
she asks me again and again i tell her that nothing is wrong

so then she goes to sleep but i stay awake
throwing our nighttime rhythm off

i'm wondering what it is we're not saying

perhaps
i don't know what i'm wondering
i just know i can't fall asleep

stirring in her sleep i reach out to her
hoping for us to nighttime kiss as we do

but she is in a sleeping state while i am awake
and our kisses which happen by themselves cannot be made

so not knowing what is going on in her mind
i wonder what is going on in her mind

we wake in the morning

and i want to tell her i love her
all i'm thinking about is how much i love her

but there's some obstacle between us
neither of us aware of what it is

she asks me what's going on
i say again that i love her

she asks what's going on
and i can't explain so i leave the room

outside the room i want to tell her i love her
so i go back inside the room

there she is and there i am
but we cannot talk to each other

so this day my brain has nothing to eat
and my brain begins eating itself

my brain eats itself at the college of the desert
during our visit to the jenny holzer exhibit

which is a fine exhibit
that i am glad we attended
though i do not act like it

i find her alone
behind our first desert x installation
superflex's *dive-in*,
where she takes a photo of us

but still during a long drive
to iván argot's *a point of view*
my brain continues eating itself

at *point of view* i find her, stand next to her

and she says she's headed someplace else

so i go to stand in the shade
under a wooden staircase
all alone because of myself

we leave and she hands me flowers
i am touched but i am confused, losing sense

everything wonderful i don't understand
and everything i imagine is all out of proportion

we stop for the international banana museum
but at the convenience store next door

a lady with a holstered gun
tells us the international banana museum
won't be opened today

so then isabelle asks me
to buy her sausages for lunch
and we pretend i'll buy her sausages for lunch

this whole time
i'm wondering what it is we're not saying

by the time she's next viewing
steve badgett & chris taylor's
terminal lake exploration platform

i'm alone inside the tourist center
which she later visits without me
because of my own decisions

arriving at the ace hotel
my brain has eaten itself

there is nothing left

my head is empty

i feel empty at the bar booth and yet
she taps the booth cushion, indicating i should
sit beside her

so then i am beside her
because she asked me to be

yet i don't know who i can be
at this particular time

which i realize
is a problem

everyone is having a good time but me
so i must be my own problem

i concentrate on fixing my problem of being me
by engaging in polite small talk

and it goes along well enough
since everyone is having a nice time

i concentrate on having a nice time
along with everyone else

a plane has three blown engines
and the cabin is on fire
can the pilot find a way to land it

walking to pia camil's *lover's rainbow*
i hold her hand

which is my favorite thing in the world
holding her hand

but it is like when in the morning

i told her i love her
she believes me but
there's something else she needs from me

later i learn she needed me in the group
that was fine while i was losing my mind

i had become the problem so
i became what was bothering her

while holding her hand as we walked
to pia camil's *lover's rainbow*

then in the night
we use phone flashlights to see an installation
sterling ruby's *specter*,
an orange monolith in the desert

i left my worries behind me at ace hotel
so i ask for a couples photo of us

me beside my favorite person in the entire world
at a desert art installation

the pilot discovers the plane's steering compo-
nents have malfunctioned
so he can't prevent
the left wing from smacking a tree

the wing falls off and the plane spins
there is nothing the pilot can do

what happens is the plane crashes
and the question is were there any survivors

everyone survived
but it was still awfully dramatic

returning back to downtown that night
just us two in the car together

i tell her i love her
and she tells me
there's something else she needs to hear

which i understand
although i don't know how to explain

isabelle in los angeles: four

i tell her i am writing poetry about her
she reads the poems

and once
she almost quotes a line from the first poem
while calling the third poem the best so far

she calls the third poem realistic
says it feels like life
(i say she likes the tension)
(it's about me being embarrassing)
she agrees the second poem was sweet
she doesn't mention the first poem right then

but she referenced a line from the first poem
about life is short
not an intentional reference perhaps
just she says that life is short
and then she remembers
a line from pablo neruda
she says the line is
"life is short, oblivion is long"

but it's "love is so short and oblivion so long"
from "i can write the saddest poem"
a poem she once sent to me
about a man whose love has moved on from him

i cannot write like pablo neruda
i cannot sound how i do not sound
i cannot dream how i do not dream
i cannot be who i am not

she had gifted me poetry books from nz,
which i adored

they were writers from nz unis,
published by unis
and writing talent does not take education
but these people had talent and education
and education is helpful

she has a masters in creative writing
and a masters in psychology
i do not have those things
others have what they have
and i have what i have
what do i have

she encourages my poetry writing
but she knows what the poems are
i know what the poems are
and i like them for that
she thinks the poems could be more but she
doesn't say it, she implies it

isabelle in los angeles: five

i am so worried about how we are
and worried about how she sees me

but then i am beside her
and still worrying about those things
but beside her
what i'm saying is
i do not worry about being beside her

isabelle in los angeles: six

i less appreciate myself when i'm around her
and a tricky thing is
some of the ways i used to appreciate myself
weren't helpful
so she's doing me a favor

i'm beginning to think at my life
rather than within it
remembering to look at the world outside me
which i feel behind about doing

she follows the proper art world
the best parts of the art world
which i used to not want to need
but this i've read and know:

men who believe they hate
what they really fear they need
are of limited interest, i find
david foster wallace, *infinite jest*

well
it is true that i did not fear the art world
but rather thought
the obscure theories of art world beauty
devour reality
but that overlooks art world beauty

she makes me feel behind on what i like
since what i've always said i like
is real people stuff

everyman art
straight from a human rather than a school
but wait do i still most like that

am i behind
or right where i need to be

here she is with me
with her own thoughts
which sound more right

when i describe what's wrong
can i make it sound right

the world as i look at it
how can i look at it deeper
while still myself
can i do this

well i can picture it
that's a step
i can describe what i need
let's see if i can achieve it

always i am calling myself impossible
i am the one calling myself impossible

isabelle in los angeles: seven

there is so much that i do not want to mention
in this poem
and every poem i write about how i felt
when next to isabelle

that whole great big world out there,
i don't need it
not when with her who will remind me about it

she reminds me of things
i hadn't thought about before

isabelle in los angeles: eight

outside our bedroom

there's a shit-ton of everything

a whole damn lot of reality

and who cares

no wait i mean

we care

about what's outside our room

and we hope that others care
about what's outside their rooms too

we hope that other people
care about other people

and here i am with her,
caring about her

here she is with me,
caring about me

vital capabilities

human possibilities

blissful actualities

she is all i need

In terms of the question in his dating service biography, "But who will write about you," now Brett could say that he had indeed written about Isabelle.

A pivotal question: would he move to Auckland/ would she move to Los Angeles?

What the hell were they doing?

The only answer they had: they could not yet dare to let go of each other.

Their immediate situation: he needed to save money to have the money to visit her, and she would be able to visit again at the end of July.

Her second visit ticket purchase came soon after her first visit since, dear reader, imagine how he felt when she told him over the phone, "I'm struggling," referring to having a hard time being away from him. Reciprocal. In the same conversation she brought up watching *Chilling Adventures of Sabrina* on Netflix, season two released that week; and taking a stroll through the city with his girlfriend on a telephone, walking up Hayworth Avenue to the building outside of which F. Scott Fitzgerald died, while being conversational Brett mentioned that day purchasing Halle Butler's *The New Me*.

The subtext was they missed each other. In the days following her first visit she would call him in her car on the way to shop somewhere for something or other, sometimes staying on the phone while shopping, sometimes shopping and then calling him again after leaving. Together how they could be together, he cherished hearing the wind against her car when she drove with him on speakerphone, and he described his reaction to the sound of her car blinker as ineffable.

He mentioned and there was veracity to the statement that although there were many perspectives from which he could describe how he loved her there was too a perspective that he could not put into words: previously referred to in this text as animal magnetism or quantum entanglement, the mysterious inability to describe its existence points toward quantum entanglement being a more accurate term to describe what kept Isabelle and Brett together (it really seems after twice considering).

Then after she had been back in New Zealand for longer and had other things to do she called him less often.

What of life transpired amid their fit of love: in-between job stints Brett began planning the production of his own new short film, *Mary was an Alien*, which was to be a sci-fi about Mary the virgin mother of

Christ having been born on another planet in another solar system. At the beginning of the six-minute short the audience learns that Mary's planet is suffering from a plague, and Mary is quarantined in a castle bedroom. Followed by this extraordinary circumstance: aliens visit Mary's planet and catch the plague, die. One night Mary escapes outside the castle to nibble freedom and by chance she discovers the alien spacecraft which by accident she activates to travel through a black hole that turns out to be a wormhole in which she becomes pregnant before crashing on Earth and giving birth to Christ. Some special effects would be necessary but Brett felt them within his reach—he knew somebody who knew somebody—so, not meaning to be sacrilegious but outrageous, he crossed his fingers about everything working out in accordance with his grand vision.

Isabelle was profiled by the country's largest newspaper, curated panels for the city's largest arts festival, sponsored a faux Bollywood film shoot that was actually a public event which went well and the local television interviewed her too, plus also she orchestrated a large-scale installation in which visitors peered through front-window portholes (circles cut into blackened windows) at artistic creations of children's dreams of a future city (for example a model of a future car). She posed in a stunning black dress for her friend's fashion label; she was dinner and drink friends with a national television news personality and several types of successful creative professionals—on a path to her own success in her home country, meeting people and making things happen. Manifesting, her dreams, she would often mention her life perspective being different from Brett's, the disparate life paths they were taking, and their dissimilar headspaces.

Isabelle was in a far different headspace when she mentioned her friend having driven a truck for her event and asked Brett, "Would you do that?" This gall from the outside reminded him that she did not consider him capable of doing all she desired to be done for her. You know: it wasn't his love bringing her the success she brought herself. Sometimes he often wondered how he mattered, which topic irritated her. Though Brett would consistently remember to mention the four things he deemed The Bare Minimums: he was proud of her, he considered her amazing, she was endlessly adorable, and he loved her.

He would tell her, "You're my everything." She
would leave that comment for a friend on social media.
He would put photos of her on his social media. She
would put photos of other people. He was becoming
familiar with her developing life that had zero to do
with him—Brett's waking nightmares were unrelated to
Isabelle's manifesting dreams. Part of Brett's waking
nightmare became Isabelle's casual decision to begin
house hunting with her flatmate best friend two-time
boyfriend whom she once mentioned she would be
friends with until death and considered a brother. She
sure seemed a lot closer to that friend than to Brett.

Brett and Isabelle broke up about three times not
when Brett learned about the house hunting but after
the thought smacked him. Could Brett and Isabelle
build a future together if they didn't build a life together? What did it mean to love somebody with whom it
felt as if you would not be able to share a life? Such
questions haunted these days. But also she had plane
tickets, and they did begin to sleep together on the
phone quite often. This was their sleeping tradition:
New Zealand was almost a day ahead—nineteen hours
ahead when it was spring in Los Angeles and fall in
New Zealand—which resulted in a five hour time dif-

ference, as in when it was eight at night in Los Angeles it would be three in the afternoon the next day in Auckland, and so when Isabelle went to sleep she called Brett while he slept, for them to sleep together, and when he woke in the morning he would sneak in a goodbye, she then being the one to return to sleep unless, if he did not happen to have work he would wait on the phone until Isabelle awoke—this ritual felt sacred to him, and she expressed her own strong feelings about the procedure that provided them long-distance relationship intimacy.

The context of life heavy, in the empty space outside of everything Isabelle and Brett loved each other: would they be able to be together? When she arrived at the end of July it was different compared to her first visit in that this time he knew that, because of love, he would feel glad to be with her no matter what. Isabelle had visited family in Singapore before this trip to Los Angeles, so upon her arrival she suffered from heavy travel fatigue and jet lag. Their Airbnb off Sunset Boulevard, Brett suggested they walk the mile and a half to Amoeba Music, because he was an idiot, who didn't realize this was a bad idea until they were halfway there, having walked past the taco truck she had wanted to go to and he had thought was somewhere further away, walking on to Amoeba before it closed. Owing to Brett being moronic, on their way back Isabelle did not desire to stop and eat, wanting to get back and sleep: understandable. Relatable. Though it was early for nighthawk Brett who had fucked up and so didn't consider it wise to lie awake next to Isabelle. Therefore Brett went outside to stroll the neighborhood, Little Armenia. He bought a tallboy from a 7-Eleven and then realized the Airbnb was near the strip club Jumbo's Clown Room, which he didn't go into, since there was a two drink minimum, and all he wanted was one more drink, so he bought another tallboy from 7-Eleven and walked around some more before heading back in for the sleep that would bring a new day, Friday, when they went to see Lulu Wang's *The Farewell* at the newly opened Alamo Drafthouse Cinema in Downtown Los Angeles. They ordered appetizers and alcohol during a movie they both very much enjoyed. Isabelle still felt jet lagged so they returned to their Airbnb for Netflix and drinks until sleep. The next night, Saturday night, they ate at El Coyote (where Sharon Tate ate before she was killed) and then they saw an opening weekend midnight screening of *Once*

Upon a Time… in Hollywood at the movie theater
Quentin Tarantino owned, New Beverly Cinema. They
sat in the front row (small side note: while leaving Brett
spotted Davey Havok also leaving). The next five
nights Isabelle and Brett spent at his place. One night
they ate at Spoon By H, a marvelous Korean restaurant
right down the street, about which Isabelle had in-
formed Brett, and then they watched *Kiki's Delivery Ser-*
vice, which instigated their nickname tradition: Kiki and
Jiji. One night one day Isabelle went alone to see a
friend for lunch (the friend having brought her own
boyfriend) and in the afternoon Isabelle and Brett went
to LACMA just to go to LACMA, then visiting the
Thai Town apartment of Isabelle's lunch friend, and
well unrelated but what ended up happening was a
fight between Isabelle and Brett over some emotional
something, resulting in Isabelle saying she was going to
stay in a hotel, and Isabelle leaving Brett's place to end
up at her friend's Thai Town apartment—the next
morning calling Brett to pick her up, which he did.
That weekend Brett drove them to their Airbnb in
Joshua Tree: a woody minimalistic place without a television but with a record player and bedside iPhone
chargers. In the middle of the desert it felt a bit like

being alone in space, except when they ate at Arby's and Applebee's. Together they watched two episodes from the new season of *Aroha Bridge* on an iPhone, and constructed a hamburger and soda meal out of powder from a Kracie Popin Cookin DIY set they purchased at Cost Plus World Market in Brett's neighborhood. She wore the black dress she had posed for in the fashion photo and hell he thought she was beautiful the entire time she was alive. The next day to their dismay two shootings with horrible overlapping details occurred: Isabelle and Brett went to Walmart, following which there was a shooting at the Walmart in El Paso, Texas, and then when going to sleep Isabelle and Brett heard about the shooting in Dayton, Ohio—the closest city to Brett's birthplace: paranormal logistics in life's harsh reality. Returning to Los Angeles they listened to several podcasts, as Isabelle was into podcasts about relationships and news and a variety of topics. On their final night they visited her friend who was also visiting, seeing Julius Onah's *Luce* with him at ArcLight Cinemas in Hollywood. What happened that night was first Brett became upset about having to pay for the friend when ordering movie tickets online, and second Brett refused when Isabelle wanted to draw money out of the ATM to repay him then. Isabelle became irate and it lingered through their last night. Brett brought up: you will be gone soon. Was this how she wanted to colonize his memories? He had intended to buy White Claws Hard Seltzer for them to drink in the alley as he sometimes did alone, but instead they went to sleep angry. Although they did cuddle in their sleep, in the middle of the night, she drew him toward her. Driving her to LAX he loved her and wondered what in the hell. She flew away and the immediate days following her New Zealand return she would call Brett and say, "I love you, baby," and he would say, "Baby, I love you." He spoke about wanting to write a script about feeling happy since because of her he felt reminded that happiness was possible in life. Although he didn't end up writing the script for the feelings he had those days.

Owing to production problems related to constructing a castle and accurately portraying space travel to the extent of his wishes, Brett found himself tragically unable to complete *Mary was an Alien*. In a chasm of frustration he felt inspired to write a three-minute short titled *Rather be a Robot than be a Human*. He could easily make this and the concept was simple: first, a futuristic newscast on the fascinating topic of developmental and cognitive robots beginning to learn about the pains of life. Over an exclusive interview an android says, "I can describe the very day, the very moment, in which I truly felt myself grow from being a robot to being alive," and okay the android would just be a human actor, a person Brett knew and had in mind, which would establish that androids look just like humans, can't tell the difference. Second, pull back from the newscast being watched by a person: the best actor Brett could find for the job, male or female, young or old. This person would be an android appearing so bummed and as if they couldn't even do anything seriously, and they would put a gun in their mouth and pull the trigger. Brett planned to spray red paint on the back wall after the gunshot, Herschell Gordon Lewis-like, but most importantly he would add in the sound effect of scrambled circuits at the time of the brain blood splatter. That sound effect, he felt in his soul, would promote the audience to consider an existential question: what about when robots feel human?

Isabelle cast the actress of a future dance choreographed live performance, *Chloe & The K-Pop Kids*. She curated panels at the nation's best literary festival and hung out with a poet whom both she and Brett admired. During a panel she hung out with another poet they both admired. She traveled to Hong Kong and mainland China for a gathering of regional art curators. Her first night away she sent Brett photos of the Hong Kong police reacting to protestors: by sheer coincidence she was near the siege of the Hong Kong Polytechnic University. The second night she sent Brett a draft of a synopsis she was writing, for a book she edited, her famous politician friend the author, and the next night Brett didn't hear from her at all, and then he heard from her less and less over the remaining days, only knowing how she was doing from photos she shared on social media. A week after she was back in New Zealand Brett would be arriving, and they had already broken up by then.

Phone sex had not felt the same until it stopped altogether. The five hour time difference and her full weekday workdays were a significant factor in the fact that she would return home from work to live and unwind with her flatmates while Brett slumbered in Los Angeles. Less and less he felt himself as part of her life, and it was about the fifth or sixth time in which a break up was mentioned that it became agreed upon by both parties then and the next day. Isabelle said she wanted to be able to buy a home with her friend, and she didn't know what Brett was becoming while making short films that nobody cared about and didn't pay his bills—the low sum he made as a production assistant unable to secure promotion, how long would that last, and what would follow? Brett couldn't fix what bothered Isabelle about him, and she couldn't fit him into a life he couldn't understand.

But they loved each other and it felt right for him to visit Auckland for a goodbye after their break up, since the relationship was ending but not the love. She did not kiss him at the airport upon pickup, which she had mentioned she would not do, he did not even try, and she did not kiss him after they had gone to Kelly Karlton's Sea Life Aquarium, which place the airplane had told him about, and she did not kiss him after she taped his absurd effort to try and pet the geese outside of Domain Wintergardens: she kissed him later at her place when they were lying on her bed, after which he asked her what it is like to be so independent, always in control of the situation, which he thought was a valid question since he did not hold it against her, but she didn't like the sound of the question, and she asked him what he knew about her, becoming rightfully mad and wanting to cancel their plans to see her one girl friend whom Brett most wanted to meet, and did get to meet, along with the friend's boyfriend, both extraordinarily nice people. But Isabelle was still frustrated by Brett when they arrived at their Airbnb apartment that had windows facing an office building, near Queens Wharf and Michael Parekowhai's *The Lighthouse: Tū Whenua-a-kura* (which they visited the following night). This night they went to bed as if sour, though they did participate in more than cuddles before sleeping. The next morning he became confused about the difference between sweet and savory while ordering a breakfast item that he regretted upon seeing, and they had brought up sharing food, which Brett mentioned, after noticing her better choice, but it came out wrong enough that she felt attacked and the whole breakfast became a minor catastrophe, only abated by she leaving to do some quick work while he walked through the rain to their Airbnb. When she returned to him in the afternoon they experienced a patch of bliss. First, she brought him to Unity Books, where he purchased Milan Kundera's *Let the Old Dead Make Room for the Young Dead*, Yūko Tsushima's *Of Dogs and Walls*,

Clarice Lispector's *Daydream and Drunkenness of a Young Lady*, and Oscar Wilde's *The Decay of Lying*. Second, upon returning to their Airbnb they drank kombucha and ate kimchi on toast, before she lay beside him playing the matching puzzle game Sumi Sumi on her phone, as he dicked around on the internet. Then she slept against his body while he watched a Netflix show describe the evolution of Hello Kitty. He was experiencing what he would call heaven. He was familiar with this heaven from when he had been resting on the pink velvet couch as she worked at the round table facing a window beyond which were the streets of Downtown Los Angeles. And when she cooked dinner for them that night in Joshua Tree. When they weren't doing much more than being together was when they would share a love energy that was obvious to anybody who could notice anything. Just being near her: absolute heaven. That night they experienced a typical disagreement owing to whether art should be perceived as time dependent and therefore ephemeral by nature, or within the framework of the whole of human consciousness spanning time, and then they ate hamburgers and watched Mati Diop's *Atlantics*. The next day they would stay at her place for one of two nights. The first night with two of her flatmates they played the board game *Catan*, which Brett had never played and thought was marvelous because of them. In this country realistic about everything but romance, that night he tossed around in bed seeking cuddles he never discovered, the next day sitting alone on a recliner reading *The Decay of Lying* in the Grey Lynn Library. Providing Isabelle space while being alone again the following day, Brett ordered a vodka and orange juice at a locally owned food place, from a worker who for some reason had never heard of a vodka and orange juice. Alone in reality, Brett visited his internet friends at a movie message board he frequented in cyberspace:

> **jenkins** [**Brett**]:   I like *Black Panther* a lot, in ways dissimilar to ways other people like *Black Panther*. And I think *Get Out* is a solid thriller, it thrilled me
> **eward**:   *Beale Street* has one of the very best scores in recent memory
> **diamonds**:   Anything James Baldwin wrote is pretty much the best
> **jenkins**:   Anyway I'm back to drinking vodka and orange juice at that place I was at the other day. Giving space. Today we leave for a beach-side home and it's exactly the kind of home in which mental breakdowns occur in movies

diamonds: I'd love to have access to booze in the library

eward: A boozy library sounds terribly appealing

jenkins: Thank you for remembering the library, that was yesterday. lol this other place happened two days ago you might have missed it, it's when I overshared the whole sitch

diamonds: All sharing is oversharing. But i don't think you're negatively oversharing for what it is worth

jenkins: She's often on her phone messaging her real friends but I shout bin

jenkins: She seduced me when we met btw

eward: The last relationship in which I was the seduced party also ended in shambles - my own fault really

jenkins: Eward it's like what a thing to learn right

eward: I've definitely had my guard up ever since then

jenkins: She's a good person btw. We're just not meant for each other, million reasons why

jenkins: I want love and she wants life experience

diamonds: That's quite a hurtful scenario

diamonds: Thing is some people can't really love without the necessary experience

Reelist: "You want an experience, go to a Jimmy Buffet concert"

jenkins: I think she loves herself btw. We just don't look at this relationship from a mature perspective

jenkins: She's hard on herself too

jenkins: It's some weird widely shared NZ trait

jenkins: They're a culture where people look at themselves as 6/10s

jenkins: They make fun of Americans for looking at themselves as 11/10s, but then they suffer that 6/10 shit so fuck them

eward: That's sad about NZ

eward: Why they so down on themselves

jenkins: It's part of their national culture

Drenk: They're the land of Hobbits and shit.

eward: Actually I was good friends for a time with an older woman in New Orleans who was from NZ, recovering heroin addict, former millionaire's wife turned waitress and aspiring screenwriter, she was brilliant but very much her own worst enemy

eward: She's remarried now and seems happy enough on social media, I hope it's an accurate representation

Drenk: Why would you grade yourself? Or theorize about the way people grade themselves? Americans are probably more obnoxious than **Drenk [Cont.]**: other people, I don't know, but there's a reason why a hegemonic superpower would be hegemonic.

jenkins: NZ is an anxious culture idk

jenkins: Nervous energy on this island country

Drenk: They're beta testing the future.

diamonds: "Competitions are for horses."

diamonds: I think it's Bartok and he's talking about comparing art, but tell NZ i said that

In the evening, with late sunsets during a December summer, Isabelle drove them to their Bethells Beach Airbnb, which turned out to be a bed and breakfast owned and operated by lovely widow-artist Mary Ann. The next day they walked to black-sand Lake Wainamu, where a bee stung the sole of Isabelle's foot, which she didn't deserve. Next they drove to Waitakere Bay where they laid in the sun, Brett covering his face with Isabelle's copy of *The New Yorker*. After which they both read on the bed, Isabelle volunteering a David Sedaris article from her copy of *The New Yorker*. Brett read what the Sedaris family thought about his longterm significant other during family vacations. Isabelle read from *Sport 47*, edited by local poet Tayi Tibble (Isabelle had gifted Brett with Tibble's *Poūkahangatus*). Then Isabelle was about to make chicken tacos for dinner and she asked Brett if he had been sharing photos of them on social media and so he asked her if she had been sharing photos of him and this started a big thing that motivated her to listen to a relationship podcast alone while making tacos. At the table together Brett said these were chicken tacos for God and Isabelle refilled her wine glass. He was staring out the window at the ocean when he said, "I'm glad to be here." She said,

"I'm glad you're here too," and so then he nearly cried, which he mentioned. They loved each other and watched Wong Kar-Wai's *Fallen Angels* until they slept, the next morning thinking about having sex before breakfast with Mary Ann, but skipping sex, not skipping a last shower together however. Back at Isabelle's place before the trip to the airport they cried and had sex. He tried to recite The Bare Minimums into her phone but failed from crying. They already missed each other. He sang her the song he would often sing her, the only song he would ever sing, "I love you/All of the time/Not just some of the time," which was a misquote of a Kind of Like Spitting song, so a line Brett wrote for Isabelle, from a melody by Kind of Like Spitting. Driving him to the airport she said, "Play our songs." Using data from a SIM card purchased at the airport, a temporary card that would soon be discarded, with plenty of data remaining, Brett played Jonathan Wilson's "Loving You." When it began Isabelle asked, "Is this one of our songs?" He nodded because it was in terms of he included it on a playlist of songs he often listened to and shared with her in the past. He mentioned, "I like the line, 'Oh, complex you,'" and he gave her a look that conveyed feeling that way about her. It really was a pretty good song in his opinion, for example the line, "To fall asleep with you/ Drift and dream with you/Where could heaven even really be if not here in this temple?" That is good stuff according to Brett's perspective. He sat on the passenger's side of the New Zealand car, so in America he would have been on the driver's side, but in New Zealand the steering wheel is on the American passenger's side. Next came "Come to Me" by Marlon Williams. Then "Loving Is Easy" by Rex Orange County. And then, of course, Faye Wong's "夢中人" played while she drove into the airport. "It's the American Airlines terminal," he said. "There's only one terminal," she said. They hugged each other and missed each other and there was not a goddamn thing they could do but say goodbye. Inside the airport he ordered KFC only because she liked that place; he sent her a photo of his chicken sandwich to flirt with her. Then they sent each other photos of each other and she texted, "I'm sorry I didn't bring you to my parents," before they texted each other I Love You I Love You I Love You until he was called for boarding.

II

Adrina You Swallow Me

Owing to only a certain number of things happening
to each person throughout their entire life, and however much happens equaling an infinitesimal amount
compared to all that will ever happen in a universe
spanning time, Brett concentrated on projecting his
imagination and sense of being into his creative en-
deavors that quenched his thirsty soul.

He felt brave with his love life in shambles. His ago-
nized feelings gifted his life a fresh perspective: what
could all else matter compared to what felt missing
from him now? Not knowing what would stir his soul
the way Isabelle had stirred his soul, Brett began to
explore his soul himself.

Rather be a Robot than be a Human was completed, it
had been made, his friend had seen it, and now Brett
wasn't sure what he could do with it. Brett had one
friend, three work friends, and knew about a dozen
other people. He did not make sense to a lot of the
people in the world who did not make sense to him.
His last success, *The World is a Universe Person* being a
Vimeo staff pick, had given him a sliver of validation
that might foster further belief in him, but *Mary was an
Alien* had proved itself impossible, and though he
made it he suspected that *Rather be a Robot than be a*

Human would not bring him recognition. He wanted recognition because he wanted to make his feature script, *Adrina You Swallow Me*, which he finished writing after returning from New Zealand (how could it matter what might be wrong with his writing when his life felt so wrong in general).

Given his cultural era and fiscal reality, Brett's short films were not shot on film but digital. His credits included: *Yesterday Is Tomorrow*, a five-minute short film about an Angeleno photographer sharing with his friend a wine-drunk idea about a shipwreck movie made from the fire's perspective—Brett had written this script for his one friend Roscoe, who made it for school; student Roscoe also directed *Holy Shit*, a Roy Andersson-like four-minute textural narrative about five young twenty-something friends manifesting finding life unreasonable by drinking beers in an afternoon parking lot, and *Cary Grant*, an eight-minute erotic short film written when Brett both felt inspired by Georges Bataille and curious about how sex cold be portrayed in cinema; *Self-Conscious Confessions*, a five-minute short film in which one actress plays seven people at a friendly nighttime social gathering—made with one stand-in and certain camera tricks, co-directed and co-written with two women; *Everything's Fine, Thanks*, a seven-minute short film about the beginning of a relationship between two young adults who deadass cannot even understand why the world exists; *Strong Men and Beautiful Women*, a six-minute short film about the ordinary lives of young men and women in Los Angeles, shot in Santa Monica, Downtown, Miracle Mile and LAX, another textural narrative; *Motor Away*, a seven-minute short film about an elderly couple who live in a motor home and seem as if stuck in life—at the end of the short the woman walks out of the motor home and the audience is supposed to wonder if she is leaving the man forever—played at the Portland International Film Festival; Brett and his work friend Tony co-directed a six-minute short film Tony edited, *Gooses*, about a teenaged midwestern girl visiting her older sister in Los Angeles—featured on a popular independent film website; and after he finished school Roscoe and Brett co-directed Brett's first foray into genre films, *Yellow Jacket Brain Fever,* a nine-minute triptych short film about a lonely middle-aged vampire hanging out one night by himself, two homeless people beginning a relationship, and a young man discovering he is a psychopathic killer; after which arrived *The Uni-*

verse is a Water Person, an eight-minute short film about a drunken man experiencing a bad night on a beach while also rescuing a person who is a sea creature which the drunken man doesn't realize.

Brett believed there were two worlds: the world we live upon (Earth) and the world we live inside (culture). He had natural ideas about combining the two, desiring for movies to evoke an outsized life that was more like a dream than most lives are. His golden rule: if one is going to imagine, imagine all the way. Imagine as hard as you can if you're going to imagine at all.

Hired by a producer acquaintance, Brett was working as a production assistant for a car commercial shooting down in Culver City when he received a call from his work friend Larry, who had read the final draft and expressed interest in producing *Adrina You Swallow Me.* (Larry had previously produced *The Universe is a Water Person.*) Brett was unable to pick up Larry's call, though Larry did leave a message in which he sounded excited asking Brett when they would be able to meet. They made plans via texts involving exclamation points.

Larry was a producer and documentary filmmaker. His recent short film he directed, *Day-Glo Daydreamers,* about alligator pet owners in Florida, premiered at the

Sundance Film Festival. To express this bluntly: Larry was capable of behaving in the adult world to a far greater capacity than Brett. Larry possessed a rational levelheaded perspective that made him adept at the same reality which suffocated Brett who felt lucky to be friends with Larry who became a creative collaborator and helped finesse the *Adrina You Swallow Me* script.

Larry's established career as a producer, his leadership role in a creative field, provided him a lucrative source of income and illustrated his business wisdom. Brett's job as a freelance production assistant required long unfulfilling hours that, on days he dedicated himself, and even on days he didn't, pushed him further away from his creative ideas that nurtured his sense of self.

That Sunday, Brett met Larry at the Kibitz Room in Brett's neighborhood. They each ordered an old fashioned and sat at a booth.

"Well," Larry said. And then he paused to, shall we say, hold a beat that would make Brett giddy with anticipation (nailed it). "Here's what I know: Jamie…" Jamie was an associate producer whom they both knew but was more of an ally to Larry: their bond deeper.

Brett was immediately super curious about, "Is Jamie still taking vision quests?"

Jamie was the kind of guy who was both a strong professional and took vision quests. Larry said, "Oh, hm. It's been a while since I heard about it, two or three weeks."

Larry continued saying what he had been trying to say, "Jamie became acquainted with a rich older man he met at the Santa Anita Park. You know how Jamie makes the crazy seem like good sense. He's become acquainted with this rich man and they do normal friend things like enjoy being around each other. And after I told Jamie about *Adrina*, get this, the rich doctor mentioned to Jamie that, if given the opportunity, he would invest in a movie young people with wild dreams want to make and nobody else will believe in. He said that!"

Emotionally speaking Brett thought Wow, as Larry and Jamie had. A Golden Ticket?

Larry said, "Thankfully, compared to this guy's age we're still young. Another thing is part of the connection between Jamie and this rich man is a shared interest in pre-code Hollywood movies." Just like Larry and Brett. "That is their favorite kind of movie, which

Jamie called to mind before bringing up *Adrina* and then, mhm, mhm, mhm," Larry nodded and smiled, "Jamie told the rich doctor that *Adrina* isn't a wild dream but a fantastic idea that somebody needs to believe in because it needs to exist!"

Larry and Brett high-fived.

"The rich man, who is a doctor, wants to learn more about us."

Brett simply flipped the fuck out inside himself: no better way to describe his reaction. He and Larry toasted and took a drink. Then Brett reached to hug Larry but knocked Larry's old fashioned down by accident. The drink spilled on Larry's pants. Why this? A song from their childhood was playing, a song from the '90s, nostalgic music now. Brett asked a bartender for a towel which Brett brought to the table before the bartender came over with a replacement old fashioned (what a nice bartender).

Brett was experienced enough at life to ask, "How interested is he?"

Larry shrugged.

"What do you think our odds are?"

"I don't think we can know."

Brett took a sip of his old fashioned.

A silent moment of mutual contemplation.

Brett noted aloud, "This is a good time for the possibility of something good in my life."

Immediately Brett thought to enlarge his statement, "Our lives."

Larry never felt bothered by the very human problem of selfishness. Just never bothered him since he related. He said, "Anytime is a good time for something good."

Brett said, "Yeah but sometimes one wonders if the good even happens."

"I always wonder, and sometimes something good happens."

They exchanged meaningful nods.

Larry and Brett finished their old fashioneds and each ordered another while sharing stories about unrelated personal life difficulties that were tangentially related if you think about it. Having talked about the things they would be doing, then they talked about who they were.

Slightly boozy from the bar, Brett's mind alive with dreams, not too boozy and on foot, returning to his apartment his script was being projected in his skull-sized hologram chamber, so he walked on for longer,

soaking up the city and believing in his dreams, pursu-
ing his exciting thought pattern in an extensive manner
before returning to his apartment for further rumina-
tion that experienced misfortune.

You see: buzzing noises started emanating from
somewhere nearby. Brett was vibing with the universe
and something like tinnitus started taking place, but
coming from a nearby fire alarm losing its battery
power or something like that. Brett wasn't sure where
the buzzing noise was coming from but he was certain
it was persistent and intrusive upon his sense of self,
altering his heartbeat and affecting his stream of
thoughts. The buzzing noise interfered with his ontol-
ogy so he went outside to search for its source. He
opened the back patio door and noticed three people
staring his way: one neighbor and two cops. They were
searching for the source as well. Brett walked to the gas
station hoping that when he returned the buzzing
would be gone. He bought Hello Panda biscuits and
returned to find the buzzing noise lingering. Why this?
He wanted to yell at an impartial reality that hadn't
meant for this disastrous overlap.

Wanting to ignore the buzzing, in order to not feel
dominated by a bossy buzzing noise, Brett turned on

music and began reading the opening of his *Adrina You Swallow Me* screenplay:

EXT. FREEWAY - MORNING

TEXT: APRIL 2

The freeway cuts through fields
that fly past the car.

PAMELA, dressed for business, drives her kid-dressed daughter
MELISSA.

Melissa holds a child's book.

Sometimes she reads the book.

The fields have cows,

Melissa notices cows in fields.

                    MELISSA
          Do you think people can learn
          a lot from cows?

Pamela glances at the cows.

                    PAMELA
          There's much to learn.

                    MELISSA
          I like how they stand there.

Pamela and Melissa ruminate.

                    PAMELA
          Have you heard the word cattle?

                    MELISSA
          No. Is it real?

                    PAMELA
          Surrre. The plural of cows is
          cattle. And well, ladies are
          cows. Can you believe it? Boys
          are bulls, probably because
          boys are bullies. And other
          words are heifers and oxen.

What else? Critters! Spooky.
Critters.

                    MELISSA
What do I call cows?

                    PAMELA
Excellent question. Stick
with "cows."

                    MELISSA
Mhmm.

                    PAMELA
We eat cows.

                    MELISSA
How?

                    PAMELA
Hamburgers. Ribs. Steaks.

Melissa watches the cows.

                    MELISSA
Wowwwww. I like cows.

Melissa reads that book of hers.

Fields fly past the car.

Pamela glances at the cows again.

                    PAMELA
          You have to hear about this
          famous old lady.

Pamela glances at Melissa.

Melissa stares at Pamela.

                    MELISSA
          I'm listening.

                    PAMELA
          She's very very very very fa-
          mous and has a successful and
          enduring song, related to be-
          cause she swallowed a fly a
          spider and a bird. Mmm. A cat,
          dog. Goat. Cow. Horse! Pheww,

                    PAMELA (CONT.)
          that horse. I tell you what,
          the horse was trouble.

                    MELISSA
          Goats are so funny. She swal-
          lowed a goat?

                    PAMELA
          She had to! She swallowed and
          ate the fly, then everyone else
          because she had to sort out her
          fly problem. Definitely. The

fly started the crisis, and
everyone died including the old
lady, who died because she ate
the horse. The horse died, ob-
viously. Andbut, the song men-
tions no one knows why things
like this happen.

                    MELISSA
Maybe we shouldn't eat cows?

                    PAMELA
Vegetarians don't, and they
tend to be quite serious people, sometimes friendly. They
can have a kinda harmony about
them. That's not me and you
though. Nope. We already have
harmony so we eat meat. We're
fine, everything's fine.
                    PAMELA (CONT.)
The worst decision the old lady
made was eating an entire horse
at once. So silly. She was silly and marvelous and a fairy
tale. We lives by this code-
word: hamburgers. Mmmmmm.
Chicken nuggets. Ahhhhh.

Melissa has a sad face.

Pamela notices Melissa's sad face.

                    PAMELA
Why do you have that sad face?

                    MELISSA
I don't have one.

                    PAMELA
Ahh you do too. I can see you
and you've got a sad face.
Please tell me why.

                    MELISSA
Can't believe I eat horses!

                    PAMELA
Nooooo, imaginary. No. Nooo.
You don't eat horses. That was
a weird old lady thing.

                    MELISSA
Are you sure?

                    PAMELA
Yep. You -- you don't eat horses or dogs. Or flies or spi-
ders. Or, mm, chinchillas or
hamsters. And you eat all kinds
of things that weren't animals
in the first place. Plants and
um, sugar.

                    MELISSA

I'm feeling worried about cows.

          PAMELA
Ohmeohmy. Cows aren't horses!
Cows are fun to eat!

          MELISSA
Doesn't sound fun to me.

          PAMELA
Oops.

Pamela rubs Melissa's knee.

Melissa gives Pamela a challenging
face.

          PAMELA
Sorry. Let's forget the old
lady. She's a bad influence.
          MELISSA
Uhhhh! I'll be reading. Secret-
ly thinking about cows.

Melissa turns back to her book.

          MELISSA
I have a few questions about
goats too.

Melissa turns back to Pamela.

          MELISSA

Saving that for another time.

Melissa turns back to her book.

> MELISSA
> Too upset right now.

EXT. MICK'S COUNTRY HOUSE - EARLY
AFTERNOON

The car stops in front of a house
alone in the country. No neighbors, no nothing of anything
around but the country.

EXT/INT. MICK'S COUNTRY HOUSE -
MINUTES LATER

Pamela bangs on the front door.
She has a frustrated face and
turns toward the front yard.

She picks up a rock from the yard
and walks back to the house.

Pamela throws the rock through a
front window that shatters.

Pamela walks to the window and
reaches in, pulls up the window
frame, and turns to Melissa.

                    PAMELA
    You stay right here.

Pamela climbs inside the house.

Melissa watches Pamela walk
through the house for about one
second.

Then Melissa walks into the front
yard.

She stares at trees, at the
ground,

she stares at the stretch of land
and the horizon,

she peeks at the sun in the sky.

She stares at everything in the
country.

She stares at her father's country
house.

This is either when we hear the
violins, or anyway when events oc-
cur which come from violins.

Melissa walks to her father's
house.

She opens the front door and walks
inside.

Pamela leans against a bedroom
doorframe, her hand over her face.
She breathes loudly, and her
breath becomes tears.

Melissa stares at her mother.

Pamela doesn't hear Melissa walk
across the hallway to her.

All the way to her.

Only through luck, pure chance,
does Pamela slam the bedroom door
shut right when Melissa is next to
her.

EXT. MICK'S COUNTRY HOUSE - AFTER-
NOON

The cop car sits next to Pamela's
car. BILL THE OFFICER stands next
to Melissa.

RONALD THE SHERIFF and Pamela
stand across from the cars,

by the front door to the house.
Pamela's back faces Melissa.

                    PAMELA
          Look at my eyes.

Pamela's eyes.

                    RONALD
          I am.

                    PAMELA
          What you're going to learn,
          it's bad. Listen. Over there is
          Melissa, Mick's daughter. This
          was Mick's house. Did you know
          him?

Ronald looks at the house while he
asks:

                    RONALD
          You mind explaining the way
          you're phrasing that question,
          ma'am?

Pamela puts her hand on her face.

                    PAMELA
          You see Melissa over there?

Ronald sees Melissa.

                    RONALD
        Yes.

                    PAMELA
        Did you know Mick?

                    RONALD
        Well, I do know him. He's a
        good man.

                    PAMELA
        He's not anymore. Please don't
        ask me what happened. You'll
        see.

                    RONALD
        I'm hearing strong words.

                    PAMELA
        His broken window—

        Pamela points to the window.

        Ronald looks at it.

                    PAMELA
        Earlier I broke it. Angry me. I
        expected Mick'd been up to mis-
        chief and was hungover. He
        tends to drink into nights,
        sleep into days. That's him and
        what he wants I guess. We di-

vorced you know. Anyway I was
mistaken, today was different,
and I didn't know his goddamn
front door was unlocked. My
bad. I broke the window. Now I
have to leave with my daughter,
and stay with her, when tonight
I'm supposed to be on a plane
to Albuquerque. Instead I'll be
home, telling her about Mick.
Her father. I'll make
up what I tell her. I can't
tell her what you'll see but
he's dead for sure.

INT. MICK'S COUNTRY HOUSE - MICK'S
BEDROOM - MINUTES LATER

Ronald by the door. His shocked
face.

Bill enters the room. His stoic
face.

Ronald's face turns to Bill.

Bill keeps staring at the bed.

Toward the bottom of the bed is
MICK'S DECAPITATED HEAD. Bill

steps forward to look at it:
Mick's eyes are missing, and the
top of his skull is removed: his
skull is empty.

Bill notices a large blue plastic
container beside the bed, inside
it blood and bones.

Bill opens a window.

EXT. MICK'S COUNTRY HOUSE - CON-
TINUOUS

This house has bad vibes. You can
feel them when you see the house.

EXT. COUNTRY ROAD - MORNING

Ronald drives his police car
through the fields. A cross dan-
gles from his rearview mirror, and
he rubs the cross with the tips of
his fingers.

EXT. SALLY'S COUNTRY HOUSE - MIN-
UTES LATER

TEXT: APRIL 11

A small house neighbors other small houses. A police car is parked in front of it.

INT. SALLY'S COUNTRY HOUSE - LIV-ING ROOM - CONTINUOUS

Mick's mother SALLY sits in a cushioned chair next to a wooden table. Ronald sits across from her. He clears his throat. Sally stares at her hands. She looks up at Ronald.

He smiles.

> SALLY
> These have been horrible times for me.

Ronald watches Sally.

> SALLY
> Well.

Sally exhales.

> SALLY
> Yup.

Sally rubs the surface of the table with the palm of her hands.

                    RONALD
    A tragedy ma'am, my sincerest
    sympathy. If I were able to
    tell you what happened I would.
    We can't put it all together.
    To be honest, ma'am, what we do
    guess I wouldn't tell you until
    we know for certain.

                    SALLY
    Awful.

                    RONALD
    More awful than awful.

Ronald scoots back his chair. He
stands.

Ronald and Sally are quiet for a
beat.

                    RONALD
    This shouldn't have happened.
    I'm a police offer so I hope
    you can trust me when I say it.

                    SALLY
    Appreciate it.

Sally looks at Ronald.

                    RONALD

Yeah.

Ronald looks at his hands.

Ronald sits back down.

                    SALLY
          For a little bit he lived with
          some woman for some time. Maybe
          for about a year up until a
          year ago. I wasn't introduced
          to her. I don't know why not
          but I know I wasn't. She
          might've been imaginary.

                    RONALD
          Jessica, you mean?

                    SALLY
          Ooh yes. Have you chatted with
          her?

                    RONALD
          I have. I didn't chat with her
          in any delicate way, no, she
          didn't much like chatting with
          me, but I chatted with her, and
          we know each other from back
          when she went to Winchill's
          while living with Mick. But.
          She doesn't know what happened

either. And she lives in Florida now.

                SALLY
 I'm so sorry.

Sally rubs the surface of the table with the palm of her hands.

                RONALD
 Mick was a mystery. A man of
 the country. You of course knew
 him much better than I did.

                SALLY
 Huh. He'd visit me about once
 or twice a month. He worried
 about his front lawn. What

            SALLY (CONT.)
 else? I suppose you already
 know about his front lawn.

                RONALD
 I've seen it.

                SALLY
 Okay.

Ronald watches Sally. Sally stares
at her hands.

                SALLY

One time, and only one time, he
told me about some woman with a
funky name. I can't remember
her funky name. Usually every
name I hear sounds like some
kind of name I'd expect to
hear, but once I heard a head
scratcher.

                    RONALD
Ma'am, it was my hope to hear
things only you'd tell me.
What's stopped you from mentioning this woman before?

                    SALLY
I'm embarrassed because I can't
remember her name.

                    RONALD
Ahh. Maybe it sounded something
like -- what would you say?

                    SALLY
That maybe it sounded like
something.

Sally looks at her hands.

                    SALLY
Maybe. I don't remember.

Ronald taps his fingertips on the
table.

                    RONALD
          When was this?

Ronald takes out his notepad.

                    SALLY
          It was about two or four months
          back I guess. I think she vis-
          ited him, and I just don't know
          for how long.

                    RONALD
          Did he say how they met, how he
          knew her?

                    SALLY
          He did not mention that. I re-
          member I don't remember the
          name of some lady who visited
          him once.

                    RONALD
          Thank you for sharing that with
          me. I'm going to write it down.

Ronald writes notes.

Ronald puts away his notepad.

> SALLY
> I'm no help. Oh, I wish I could
> be, since he's dead. But I have
> a bad memory.

> RONALD
> You remember Mick?

Sally looks at Ronald.

> SALLY
> I remember my own son, but not
> as well as you or I wish.

> RONALD
> Remember him at all. I will. He
> was my friend and I'll remember
> every part of him I knew. He
> was a good person.

Sally looks at her hands.

Ronald stands. He puts his hand on
Sally's shoulder.

> RONALD
> I don't have any more ques-
> tions. Except, well. Is it true
> that Mick loved peanut butter?

> SALLY
> Quite true.

```
Ronald walks away.

          RONALD
   I'll give you answers when I
   can. Wait and hope.

          SALLY
   Okay sure but for now I'm going
   to take a nap.
```

The buzzing noise that was more specifically similar to a screeching noise would vanish and reappear, come and go, the music always playing and Brett always reading these pages that could put his thoughts in a safe place if not for the screeching noise—while reading the pages he saw himself doing what he wanted to do: creating what he wanted to create.

But was he creating to his furthest extent? It felt alive and full of character, to him, and he hoped it would for others, but also he hoped for more than life and character. Reality alone did not interest him, the feeling of it did.

Ah, this was a beginning part, and Brett was aware of and liked what he was building up to. He felt this opening would keep the audience guessing what might happen. He wanted to evoke feelings of spontaneity and provoke surprise. Yes, he decided to like what he had written. He hoped he was entering a new phase of his life and that the screeching noise would stop soon. That somebody would find the source of the screeching and shut it off please. His New Zealand visit had been six weeks prior. During their relationship, Isabelle would very often call to say she loved Brett during the month following seeing him, and much less after that —during Isabelle's frequent calls she would ask if the frequency bothered Brett, and of course he said and meant that no it did not bother him, for he treasured it while knowing the frequency would fade, as it did each time—and now their relationship over, after he left from New Zealand she texted him with sporadic messages of love and longing for about a month, a little over a month because she mailed him birthday presents (facial moisturizer, a box of LCMs, and a poetry book titled *I Thought We'd Be Famous*), and he echoed her sentiments, but not her finesse, having not sent her a birthday gift, neither of them having given each other Christmas presents—the birthday presents had been a nice last touch that further revealed a side of her lighter than him—though he knew her messages would fade, which they did as time moved on, followed by the same kicker as in their relationship: they lost their sync; and in her absence he missed her, to the extent that that was when he missed her the most, but in this situation Isabelle's frequent calls would not be returning. The meeting with the rich doctor was scheduled for approximately a month after the meeting with Larry for your information, and in the days leading up to it Brett racked his brain about the best way to present *Adrina*, discussing with Larry what their most advantageous tactic might be. They rehearsed their presentation in Larry's living room, with Brian Eno music providing a nurturing creative atmosphere—Brett owned a plant named Brian Eno, which Isabelle had gifted him: that is how this detail has been included in the narrative—Brett and Larry agreed that during their presentation Brett would be the emotional angle and Larry would handle logistics.

Brett had three freelance art department production assistant jobs, thirteen work days, between the meeting with Larry and the presentation. Outside work, Brett spent his extra time strategizing with Larry, and being alone while ruminating upon his past and future as usual, except once visiting his one friend whom he routinely saw every month or so, and chatting with another work friend for topical purposes.

The work friend he chatted with was Tony, who was not an active true friend, and yet remained a vital work friend. Tony possessed celluloid semen and longed to become the Mr. Rogers of sex films: he made complete sense to Brett from a philosophical cinematic perspective. They were romantic cinephiles whose lives felt blessed by significant others and significant movies; they each adored movies that felt as if somebody's soul had exploded in the making.

Tony was from Chicago, Illinois, but met Brett while teaching in Portland, Oregon, back in the two years when Brett had lived in Portland (which felt too tiny compared to Los Angeles in his opinion). Tony had been taught editing at a film school in London, England, and was Brett's teacher at the Northwest Film Center. Many fellow editing students searched for logistics, but Brett took Tony's class for spiritual reasons that truly related to what Tony really wanted to discuss it just so happened.

Tony showed the class the opening of *Silent Light*, written/directed by Carlos Reygadas, for spiritual purposes. Nobody in the class wanted to make anything remotely similar to *Silent Light*, but both Tony and Brett treasured expansive cinematic forms. Tony wanted to speak about the soul of cinema when he showed scenes from Vera Chytilová's *Daisies*, and only Brett thought: totally. They so understood each other they became friends outside of class, and decade-older Tony showed Brett a laserdisc edition of the anime masterpiece *Akira*, a torrented copy of Robert Jan Westdijk's home-movie-like *Zusje*, and a dvd of the contemporary arthouse movie *Innocence* by Lucile Hadzihalilovic. On top of which, one time Tony sponsored a neighborhood theater film print screening of Frank Zappa's *200 Motels*, the first movie shot on tape. And at the same neighborhood theater another time, and many times later, around the time of his birthday Tony showed a film print of Radley Metzger's porn chic *Score*, with a chest of costumes at the front of the theater, for the audience to dress up when the movie characters dress up. The theater was closed to the public, only friends, and a Madonna-themed birthday dance party followed the movie. And as a teacher, through the school, Tony promoted a film print screening of Richard Lester's *The Knack ...and How to Get It*, at the Whitsell Auditorium in the Portland Art Museum: Tony and Brett sat in the front row.

Just to go on and on about it: the concept of cinema blossomed in the mind of Brett, and he discovered expansive cinematic possibilities on his own too. His eyes first opened to contemporary arthouse cinema through Nuri Bilge Ceylan's *Distant*: Mahmut's discontent with Yusuf felt palpable to Brett, and what Brett's younger self considered arthouse nonsense became comprehensible expressions of deeper needs (Brett's favorite topic)—it just clicked for him: unspoken internal narratives, the existential as the exterior, and a cinematic tapestry of reality. Though Brett did think that modern stuff exaggerated itself by acting like the future. Every past was once a future, everything is the past upon completion, every today is tomorrow's nostalgia, and Brett preferred what transcended time. He didn't want to feel fond of the past, he wanted to experience it as the present. As he remembered experienc-

ing *Distant*, so too he remembered when he first experienced Rouben Mamoulian's *Love Me Tonight*. Brett's
favorite movies about reality were directed by Yasujirô
Ozu and Edward Yang, his preferred movie franchise
was Godard in the '60s, his cherished trilogy was *Apu*,
and certainly he didn't think of cinema as just his favorite childhood movies, or what was playing at the
multiplex over the weekend—he thought of cinema as
a beautiful whole composed of everything from
everywhere and anytime, and it all felt significant to
him, he wanted everything.

Tony and Brett were not the only people who ever
had or ever would feel spiritual about movies, just they
were the people most like this that they each knew at
the time they were friends. So, owing to organic chem-
istry, Tony and Brett were true friends for a short
while, but emotional technical difficulties rewired them
into work friends, and any-way Brett touch based with
Tony about *Adrina*. Tony said he would edit a feature
film for the person whose cinematic philosophy he
understood, if such a situation arose: a wholesome mu-
tually appreciative texting conversation between Tony
and Brett one night, which Brett counted as meeting

with Tony based on how rare it was for him to interact with anybody in any way honestly.

There was a full moon the night Jamie drove Larry and Brett out to a well-endowed house in Hollywood Hills, in order to meet the rich man. The rich doctor answered the door. Brett pretended he felt relaxed and comfortable. The rich man said he was glad to see them, and led them across a marbled hallway, toward a pearl colored carpeted room, with two pink velvet recliners and a pink velvet couch. The rich man sat on a recliner and motioned to the couch and other recliner. Jamie sat on the recliner and Larry and Brett sat beside each other on the couch.

The rich man said, "Gentlemen, let us get to know each other after I get to know about the movie. Let us begin not with friendship but business."

That was so adult of him, Brett thought right away. He glanced at Larry who was somehow nodding and smiling as if he felt that was a natural thing for somebody to say. Larry said, "Excellent."

Larry provided a short introduction about his history with Brett and their production experience. "We've worked to become who we are. We're capable people.

We're knowledgable people. And we can make the movie we'll describe tonight."

Then it was Brett's turn, as rehearsed. He felt nervous and said, "Look at your hand, and picture a penny on it." The rich man did not look at his hand. "And then close your eyes." Brett nodded and waited while the rich man did neither thing. Brett was unsure about quite how to react so he looked at his own hand and closed his own eyes. After a brief moment he opened his eyes and the rich man's eyes were still open. Brett said, "First look at your hand and picture a penny on it, and then close your eyes please." The rich man titled his head and then did close his eyes (without glancing at his hand). Brett said, "You can trust me. I can guide you. Let yourself trust me. Be guided by my voice. This is ahead of you: when you open your eyes, where there was once a penny, now there will be a hundred dollar bill. Open your eyes and trust me, see a hundred dollar bill." The old man opened his eyes and without even glancing at his hand he initiated intense prolonged eye contact with Brett. Brett continued, "And tonight Larry and I are going to tell you about our movie concept *Adrina You Swallow Me*, but let me mention, allow me to mention please, that as well as we tell you about this, the concept is for a movie that will be like the penny which became a hundred dollar bill after you trusted me."

Brett had not delivered this as well as he had wanted to, or actually it had not been a smart idea in the first place, and his manner of speech often made his rehearsal apparent. His voice had lost a proper emotional wavelength and he sounded rehearsed which felt awful. The rich man did not make any facial gestures or perform indicative body behavior. It was Larry's turn to speak.

"Thank you, Brett. Now, Brett and I don't think that contemporary Hollywood movies suck. We just think it sucks to watch a lot of contemporary Hollywood movies. We don't want a picture of reality, we want the feeling of it. We want to be inside our movies: live on the screen. When reality becomes a movie tremendous things can happen, and that's the kind of movie we want to make."

Next Larry provided a four minute synopsis for *Adrina You Swallow Me*; Brett watched the rich man listen and sip from a glass of bourbon whiskey on the rocks.

Following Larry providing the synopsis, it was Brett's turn again. "A tale of dark hope. A particular human experience that feels like nightmares realized. People like to be around people but sometimes a social reality is disappointing, so people also like to be around movies that feel like people." That sounded off? Brett glanced at Larry for help, forgetting his mental trajectory: oops.

Part of what the rich man liked was the attention of visitors appreciating his taste. His perspective mattered tonight and Larry knew how to feed into that, based on Larry being adept at the adult world as has been mentioned. "We've heard that you, Dr. Aira, are a consumer of the essential, as we are. We are lucky to be meeting with you, and we too have hungry souls nourished by cinema. We, as you, experience ecstasy from movies with veins visible beneath the photography. And as Brett mentioned, if *Adrina You Swallow Me* sounds good to you—"

A pause for dramatic effect (classic Larry).

"—it will be better than you are even imagining. We know how to put this together. We know what we have to do and we want to do it. Thank you for your time and interest. Ask us anything."

"Thank you," Brett said. "Ask us anything."

Jamie had been watching from the recliner in a friendly way the whole time but the room felt stale after their conclusion regardless. Larry and Brett did not feel as if they had pulled off anything, though they wished to be incorrect about that perspective.

"Thank you, boys, both of you," Dr. Aira said. "I have one question: do you feel that this needs to be made, and that the world would be at a loss without it?"

Brett said, "Yes."

Larry said, "Yes."

Dr. Aira leaned forward and said, "Why?"

Jamie slapped his armrest and said, "That's two questions."

Dr. Aira didn't flinch and said, "It's the same question."

Brett felt called into action while nervous still. He said, "Listen: our lives, every moment is gone from us as it happens. Once a movie is made, it remains the same while we change. Movies are eternal. We understand that and want to make a movie."

Larry nodded, nodded. He said, "Ours are classic materials with a fresh spin: a romantic and macabre story about personal agency. It'll be a genre movie and genre movies always sell. But also we think it can move people in a way that other genre movies don't. It will be its own type of movie amid the masses."

Dr. Aira said, "Fantastic," without making a revealing facial expression.

Next life became slow-mo for Brett while Dr. Aira described his history with Jamie which Brett already knew. Brett's thoughts became trapped in his lifelong riddle about whether his perspective of the world was beneficial to a perception of the world. If he mattered. In his cultural era silenced cultures were finding voices. White cisgender hetero men had not been the silenced. Dr. Aira was an Argentinian who became friends with Jamie but still Brett could not know Dr. Aira's perspective on this issue. Parallel to this topic was the topic of whether Dr. Aira had sensed possibilities within the movie in general. Whether Larry and Brett had sounded centered within a swirl of life's variables, and able to form a meaningful pattern amid infinity. Loving cinema is different from being able to create a movie. Had Larry and Brett properly expressed their production capabilities? How misguided their rehearsals seemed now. How unfortunate Brett's beginning seemed to him. They had perhaps wanted the grander of their hope to inspire grand beliefs in the movie. But reality is far more complicated than one's hopes. They could believe in themselves but success requires much more than a belief in oneself: Brett had this on his mind while Dr. Aira walked them to the door and said good-night.

Though Brett did not leave feeling melodramatic or tragic, for he did not know what the narrative would become. The weight of life did not weaken him because some human part of him was strong enough to hold it. Sometimes he failed himself in this capacity but life experience had confirmed to Brett that the world is hard enough without you being hard on yourself. Even if he was doing it all wrong, still, he was doing it. Always forward.

That night before sleep, a citizen of cinema, he began Hu Bo's *An Elephant Sitting Still*, which he would finish in increments over a series of nights. To him it further opened a concept of what cinema could be, in terms of what it could feel like. A citizen of literature, he started reading Harry Dodge's *My Meteorite: Or, Without the Random There Can Be No New Thing*, not from the first page to the last page but in scrumptious sections. Brett felt himself sharing certain life curiosi-

ties and interests with Harry Dodge, including ones
related to the capabilities of writing: how and why
writing happens.

  Brett favored going out in public by staying in alone
and reading or watching a movie, and Dr. Aira's pend-
ing response to the *Adrina* presentation soothed Brett
with a positive sense of mystery about what might
happen in life. Not allowing himself to expect failure,
he allowed himself the pleasure of imagining himself
becoming able to create a feature length motion picture. That it was possible for him. And he watched
Hong Sangsoo's *Hotel By The River*: there was life, right
there on a screen. Ninety-six minutes of reality. He
read *The Golden Ass* by Apuleius and felt lifted by the
past. How outrageous a novel, and how glad Brett was
that it had endured so that he could read it hundreds
of years after it was written. He finished *The Golden Ass*
a day before he heard from Larry that Dr. Aira very
much liked their presentation but realized that financ-
ing a movie had been a whimsical thought of his—it
was just not his thing and it wasn't personal.

  Nobody tends to turn somebody down on purpose,
in this situation not being personal meant not being
possible. Dr. Aira said he thinks *Adrina* should be

made but it really couldn't be financed by him he realized after he stopped to think about it.

Larry said they would still keep going. But, go where? Brett thought: now this is my reality. Now this was Brett's life's circumstance: everything the same. Could anything change? He could give up on himself but why, no not that kind of change.

He couldn't read or watch a movie to find the strength to defeat his despair these days. He wasn't finding new ideas within himself while lost in what's called the fog: when all of life feels like so much that you can't see through it, you can't even see yourself within in it and you don't know where you're going. Again, that's called the fog and Brett was stuck in it as time moved forward while he felt lost. He worked as an art department production assistant on a promo for a bad horror movie and he thought: this is my life? This is what's happening to me, he wondered to himself while not seeming to like his job and leaving a bad impression on everyone around him who was fighting their own fight and needed team strength. When somebody feels stuck, everybody feels stuck with them. After a while Brett felt used to the fog and he hadn't wanted or intended for this to happen but it did. The fog became the place he was used to, the only place he knew those days.

If one should succeed in either love or business, Brett wasn't succeeding in general. And the *Adrina You Swallow Me* script remained the same. We may change, but the written remains the same. Still Brett had written *Adrina* and liked what he wrote. He understood why he wrote it and why he felt inspired to finish it after returning from New Zealand. His movie concept made artistic sense to his emotional reality and he remembered that the world he lived upon was different from the world he lived inside. He was not back with Isabelle, but the script to *Adrina* was always his.

The first twelve script pages, shared here previously, described Mick's daughter and ex-wife notifying the police after discovering his ravaged body. The vibe is meant to be gothic misery. The sheriff has a pitiful conversation with Mick's mother in a dilapidated house. It's drenched in feelings of death and decay. And the audience is meant to be learning about a narrative meant to be opening unto them. The audience member no doubt already thinks about a person named Adrina, based on the title, and they have seen a killing, but they might wonder what kind of killing have they seen.

Following the Mick sequence is the introduction of an elderly New Aged woman of color. Picture: candles, chakra, astrology, cats, and all her best friends are fascinating people. She lives in some small-town leftwing California place. There is a scene with her and her female friends—a nice quiet night in which they discuss books and movies they've read and art they've seen and things they've done recently. But the woman's face is serious too. She gives her three cats to a friend. The friend asks why. She won't say. After her friends leave she cleans the table, dusts some shelves, and leaves a plate of cookies on the table. Her favorite music plays: the music she listens to when she can choose what she listens to.

Her doorbell rings.

Cut to a phone screen and news of the woman's death. An anchorman shares speculation about a cannibal serial killer. We're in a cafe in Downtown Los Angeles. Mainly men visit here. There is a "regular day" scene: guys immersed in the concerns of their own lives sitting alone at tables, eight disparate types of men in a quiet cafe.

About two minutes of that. A lingering image. The audience almost feels as if watching security camera footage. It's a bunch of people doing nothing in particular, although everything the people do has everything to do with them.

Then the sheriff from the beginning of the movie, Ronald, is on the phone. He says "I'll be right there." And he gets in his car and drives southwest to Los Angeles. He lifts police tape and enters the cafe. Inside are 5-6 "large blue plastic containers" similar to the container seen at Mick's. There are bones and things in the blue containers, but the rest of the cafe is clean as a whistle. "Expository cop talk" explaining there's a clear connection to this and the Mick murder. They attempt to use a cop perspective to guess what's happening but they feel lost about what type of person would want to do this and why.

The audience has seen Mick, the elderly New Aged woman, and a cafe of eight single men (including the cafe owner). Adrina has not yet been introduced, for she is being saved à la Orson Welles in *The Third Man*. The audience is being seduced by the idea of Adrina.

Then enters Samuel Bink and his blue-collar life. He's a mostly nonemotional, rugged, man-type character.

Basically, an Ernest Hemingway tip of the iceberg type. We become introduced to Sam's life and learn about normal life stuff related to the life of Sam. Such as when he is fired from his job and unsure about what his next job might be. How he eats out alone and goes home alone. How he walks his neighborhood sidewalks alone and et cetera related to a lonely life. He is balding. His teeth are yellow. He does not resemble what one might call a Hollywood actor. Neither does his life. This is Brett's horror movie and in it life does feel like a horror. But this is a perspective, this is a creation. This is being imagined. Sensationalized for honesty. It's melodramatic.

In order to establish a broader context of the problem, since Brett can guess that some in the audience might be thinking that money is the problem, Sam will be sitting in the living room watching the news and the anchor will say, "Millionaire entrepreneur Laura Rivera is the latest victim of the Cannibal Serial Killer. Her skeletal remains were discovered in her San Clemente yacht." You introduce this rich person because many people prefer to think about rich people. Many people would prefer to be like rich people. In this movie it's meant to be that everybody is only themselves, and the environments that might look and sound sad only seem sad because murders take place. The environment isn't creating the reality, the murder narrative is. Brett mentioned a rich person so the audience members who like rich people could know this happens to rich people too.

   We see Sam drive down the 405, and watch him pull into an Oceanside exit. He checks into a bed and breakfast. He sits out on a front balcony and watches the ocean. She appears on the balcony. He says, "Adrina." Their eyes lock, and seeing them see each other, one can feel the magnificence they feel. They leave to have dinner together in Oceanside. A Thai place. Adrina orders pad kee mao. Sam orders pad see ewe. They return to their room and Sam plays a song on a guitar. The song "Truly Great Thing" by Sebadoh. Sam is not a musician but learned this song to play it now. The song concluded, he puts down the guitar. He says to Adrina, "Do you mind—I don't quite know how to tell you I'm ready to be prepared." She says, "Let us visit the ocean at night." They make love through sunset. Holding each other after sundown, he says, "It is you whom I have waited for my entire life." She begins to cry. He cries too. A full moon rises before they arrive at

a secluded beach. There will be no blue plastic container this time. This happens during low tide and she
cooks over a fire what meat of his she does not take
for later. The ocean will cover the mess. She releases
his bones into the water. This is one that goes off the
record. Never known by Sheriff Ronald or others.
Confessed by nobody. And only one person could have
confessed, but her secrets with others were never discovered. Always a mystery to those on the outside: Adrina, who meant much to the few who knew her. She
gave them their dream love. Some might say that it was
not what these people should have wanted, some
might call them Adrina's victims, but those who would
say such things forget that love is not a matter of what
one wants, but what one needs. And for them, they
wanted to live but they needed to die. Adrina understood. Everything else around them didn't matter when
you look right at the fact that they got from her the
one thing they wanted more than anything else. They
thought of it as dying while touching the light.